D0265031

This Book
Belongs To:

....

....

Magical Stories

Magical Stories

Illustrated by Claire Henley

This edition published by Parragon in 2011

Parragon
Queen Street House
4 Queen Street
Bath BA1 1HE, UK

ISBN 978-1-4454-1981-7

Printed in China

Contents

Rocky Finds a New Job

"Hooray! It's Saturday!" yelled Tom and Jenny as they ran up to the little café in the park, where Rocky the Dinosaur sold ice creams.

Everyone liked Rocky and he was always happy, serving all the children in the café.

After an ice lolly each, Tom and Jenny played on the roundabout.

"Wheee!" they yelled excitedly, as they spun round.

Just then, Mr Gribble the park keeper put a sign on the climbing frame.

"Sorry kids," he said, "this frame isn't safe any more, but don't worry, we're getting a fancy new one next week!"

Jenny and Tom went to tell Rocky the exciting news, and eventually found Rocky sitting alone on a bench, looking miserable.

"What's wrong, Rocky?" they asked.

"Well, the new climbing frame is very expensive. There's not enough money to buy it and keep the café open as well. So I have to look for a new job," replied Rocky, looking even sadder.

"We'll miss you so much," said Jenny, almost crying.

Luckily, on his way home, Rocky passed the local museum, where they needed a dinosaur for a new exhibit.

"It doesn't sound as fun as the café," thought Rocky. "But I'll give it a go, anyway."

The next week, Tom and Jenny went to the park. The new climbing frame was coming that very afternoon.

All of a sudden, Mr Gribble came rushing up. "Something terrible has happened!" he said.

"What's wrong?" asked Tom and Jenny.

"I've just heard that the new climbing frame has fallen apart. It's completely useless! Everyone will be so upset!" he said unhappily.

Just then, Tom had an idea. He grabbed Jenny by the hand.

They raced into town, and ran straight into the museum. They found Rocky standing very still in one of the rooms.

Rocky's eyes lit up when he saw Tom and Jenny.

"Hello, Tom! Hello, Jenny!" he exclaimed. "What are you doing here?"

"Come with us, we've got an idea!" said Tom, quickly grabbing Rocky's hand, as people looked on in amazement.

Back at the park, the children ran straight up to Mr Gribble.

"I've had a great idea!" said Tom. "Why can't Rocky be our new climbing frame?"

"Oh, please!" cried Jenny. "It's a brilliant idea, and will make everyone so happy."

They waited for his answer, hardly daring to breathe.

"I think it's a wonderful idea, too," said Mr Gribble. "Welcome back, Rocky!"

Everyone cheered loudly, especially Rocky.

Molly and Moonlight

Of all her toys, Molly's favourite was her little horse, Moonlight. She was pale silver, and her eyes sparkled like stars.

Molly and Moonlight had wonderful pretend adventures.

Molly loved Moonlight. But more than anything, she wished that Moonlight could be a real pony, who would prance and gallop and take her on real adventures.

One night, not long after Molly fell asleep, a soft whooshing noise woke her up. She sat up in bed and saw that her window was open, and the wind was blowing the curtain.

In the shimmering moonlight, Molly noticed something that made her heart stop...

Moonlight was gone!

Jumping out of bed, Molly rushed to the window and looked out.

She could hardly believe her eyes! There, prancing around the apple tree in the middle of the garden, was Moonlight.

Filled with wonder and excitement, Molly rushed downstairs. She let herself out of the back door and ran into the garden.

With Molly on her back, Moonlight trotted around the garden. Then she began to gallop and, with a quick leap, sailed over the garden fence.

Molly held her breath and clung to Moonlight's silver mane as they galloped.

Suddenly, it felt as if Moonlight was galloping on the wind itself.

Looking down, Molly realized that they were flying in the wind, across the midnight sky.

Higher and higher they flew, above the rooftops and treetops. The full moon cast its silvery beams, and all around them the stars twinkled merrily.

With a prance, Moonlight took Molly swooping through the stars and clouds. They leapt over moonbeams, darted between shooting stars and raced around planets.

When the first light of dawn began painting the sky pink, Molly knew it was time to go home.

Moonlight flew down, into the garden and in through Molly's bedroom window.

Molly crawled into bed, and fell fast asleep.

Soon sunlight was streaming through the window, and Molly's mum was calling from downstairs.

"Molly, it's time to get up!"

Molly looked over at the window-sill. There was Moonlight, just where she always was.

"Was I just dreaming?" Molly wondered. She rushed to the window and looked down into the garden. Everything looked the same, but...were those really hoofprints around the apple tree?

Molly looked at Moonlight. Maybe it was the breeze blowing Moonlight's mane, or maybe Molly's eyes were playing tricks on her. But she was sure Moonlight was gently nodding at her!

No Such Thing as Magic

Joshua looked like an ordinary little boy. But Joshua wasn't ordinary at all. You see, Joshua was a wizard. A wizard who could do all sorts of magical things... like turning dogs into toads, and cabbages into cakes!

Joshua always tried his best to show his mum and dad what a wonderful wizard he was, but they were usually too busy being grown-ups to take any notice.

And whenever they did notice, they'd always say, with a laugh,

"Joshua, don't be daft. There's no such thing as magic!"

Not even Joshua's friends believed he was a wizard.

They thought he was joking. Even when he made scrummy cakes and sandwiches appear for them to eat.

Then, on Joshua's birthday, he had a huge party at his house with all his friends.

"I'll show you I'm a wizard," cried Joshua. "I'll change Mum's party food into a feast."

Throwing his arms wide open, Joshua shouted, "Abracadabra!"

In a flash, the table was piled high with lots of shiny sweets, cream-filled buns and wobbly jellies. At the centre of the table stood an enormous chocolate-covered birthday cake.

"Yesssss!" cried all the children, tucking in greedily.

"Wow," burped Sam. "So you really are a wizard, after all."

"Yes," replied Joshua, looking very pleased with himself. "And to prove it even more, I'm going to bring in some of my special friends."

Joshua stood back and clapped his hands three times. In a puff of magic smoke, Martha the Monster and Dermot the Dragon appeared before them. Martha and Dermot were the cuddliest, friendliest, nicest creatures you could wish to meet, and before long, everyone was getting on very well.

Dermot had a brilliant time giving the children rides around the room, and then Martha showed them all how to do the monster stomp.

Everyone squealed with laughter as they thumped around the dining room while Dermot tapped out the beat with his tail.

Then, suddenly, above all the noise, Joshua heard a door bang. His mum was coming back. Quick as a flash, he clapped his hands and Martha and Dermot disappeared. By the time the door swung open, all the children were sitting back around the table once more.

"What was all that noise about?" frowned Mum.

"Nothing," cried all the children at once.

And Mum soon forgot all about the noise when she saw their empty plates. "Brilliant," she beamed. "Looks like you all enjoyed that."

"Yes," cried Joshua and his friends. They certainly had enjoyed their magical afternoon.

And from that day on, Joshua's friends never forgot that he was an amazing wizard. But they all agreed that the grown-ups should never be told, because, after all, grown-ups think "there's no such thing as magic!"

Elephant Has a Cold

It was a peaceful morning in the jungle. Everything was calm and quiet. Until… AH-CHOO-BOOOOOM!

The loud crash echoed through the jungle, rattling the treetops and making the ground tremble. Coconuts toppled down and rolled everywhere.

It happened again and again. Trees shook, and large rocks began sliding into the river.

"This is awful!" said Hippo.

"We have to cure Elephant's cold," said Giraffe.

"Warm coconut milk can be very soothing," said Monkey, opening a coconut.

Elephant stuck out his trunk and tried to drink some of the milk.

Slip-slurp…

AH-CHOO-BOOOOM!

A great big sneeze sent the coconut milk flying, splashing over everyone else.

Elephant sniffled miserably. "I've nebber had a tode before," he said.

"I dust want to feel bedder!"

"Why don't you try a nice soothing mud bath?" asked Hippo.

Everyone thought that sounded like a good idea.

"Berry relaxig!" said Elephant, as he sank into the squidgy mud.

Everyone else was beginning to relax, too, as they watched Elephant sink down deeper into the mud with a happy smile on his face.

"Ahhh," sighed Elephant contentedly. "Ahhh... ahhh... AH-CHOO-BOOOOOM!"

Elephant's sneeze splattered mud all over his friends.

"It's no use," said Parrot, shaking the mud out of her feathers. "We'll have to call Dr Lion."

"Where's the patient?" Dr Lion asked importantly, when he arrived. The animals led him to Elephant, who was sitting miserably with some palm leaves wrapped around his trunk.

"Hmmm..." said Dr Lion, listening to Elephant's chest.

"Say ahhh," said Dr Lion, looking at Elephant's throat.

"I see," said Dr Lion, looking in Elephant's ears. "Yes, indeed," said Dr Lion, looking down Elephant's trunk.

"Well," said Dr Lion, after he had finished examining Elephant, "the only thing that will cure Elephant's bad cold is..."

The other animals came closer to listen.

"...rest!" announced Dr Lion. "Lots of rest is the only cure for a cold in the trunk."

As soon as Dr Lion left, Elephant fell fast asleep. He slept for the rest of the day... and all that night... and all the next day and night, too.

His friends took turns sitting with him so they could be sure he was all right. He snuffled and snorted and snored, but he didn't sneeze. Not once!

On the third morning, Elephant woke up, stretched his trunk, and took a deep breath...

"Ah... ah..."

All his friends held their breath...

"...Aaaaaaahhhh! I feel SO much better!" Elephant announced.

The other animals cheered and hugged Elephant.

"We're so glad!" they said.

"Thank you all for looking after me," said Elephant. "You've been such good friends. And, of course, I would do the same for you if any of you had a cold!"

"That's good," said Parrot, "because I think... SQUAWK-CHOOOOOO! I may be next!"

The Remembering Fairy

Georgina's mum was terribly forgetful. Every day she would forget something important. Sometimes, she even forgot to wake Georgina up!

One particular day, Georgina was feeling very miserable. Mum had forgotten that today was Fancy-Dress Day, and had not made Georgina a costume.

The other children came to nursery dressed as clowns and ballerinas, or as wild animals and monsters.

Georgina was just wearing normal clothes!

"I wish there was a way I could make Mum remember things," she said sadly.

Suddenly, there was a puff of smoke and sparkle.

"I'm the Remembering Fairy," said a little voice, "and I'm here to help."

"But how can you help?" asked Georgina, feeling very confused.

"I help people like your mum remember things," said the fairy. "So, next time your mum is about to forget something, I'll be there!"

"Thank you," said Georgina.

The fairy smiled, and disappeared in another puff of smoke and sparkle.

"Well," thought Georgina, "what a helpful fairy."

Next morning, Georgina came down to breakfast. She was surprised to see Mum waiting for her with her bag already packed.

The next few days were the same. Every time Mum had something important to remember, the Remembering Fairy popped up and whispered in her ear.

After two weeks with the Remembering Fairy, Georgina's mum found she was starting to remember things more and more.

"You know," said Mum, "I really think my memory is getting much better."

Georgina heard a familiar puff of smoke and sparkle near her ear.

"Well, Georgina," whispered the fairy, "I think my job here is done."

Georgina smiled. "Mum does seem really good at remembering things now. Thank you so much, Fairy."

"I'm pleased to help," said the fairy, and in a flash she was gone.

Georgina hasn't seen the fairy again since, but she always keeps an eye out for that special puff of smoke and sparkle – she certainly won't forget the Remembering Fairy!